11

Once upon a time there was this monster and he lived with this little boy. They started reading and writing.

Monster wrote out the invitations for his birthday party and the little boy helped him.
And now they've finished the invitations.

Monster rolled out the pastry to make biscuits and other things for the party.
Monster made a monster cake.
The little boy said,
"Don't make a monster cake,
make a birthday cake."
So he did.

They put icing on the cake.
The boy put flowers
on the cake and
Monster put patterns on it.
It was a gigantic cake.

They decorated the walls with
balloons and streamers.
The little boy helped Monster.

Then they started sending out
the cards to
the mothers and fathers.
They thought all the children
would come.
Monster was laughing.

The mother said, "You can't go
to Monster's because he might
eat you up. You cannot go to a
monster party. The answer
is no—absolutely not.
The answer is absolutely not."

The boy said, "Daddy, Daddy,
can I go to a monster party?"
"Why go to a monster party?
The monster might eat you up
and chop you to bits. No,
you may not go to the party."

No one came to the birthday
party and the little boy was sad.
Monster was very sad. Nobody
came to his party.
Monster said, "We will have to
eat up the cake all by ourselves
instead of having the children
help us eat up the cake and
ice cream."
Boy! Did Monster have a sad
face that day.

Then there was a fire. Smoke was coming out of the building. All of a sudden fire was bursting out of the windows. People were in that building.

Monster said to himself, "Somebody's going to get killed in that burning fire."

People ran out to see the fire.
All the people were looking.
Then Monster came. He had a
very magic umbrella.

He just let the umbrella go up.
He told all the people to slide
down the umbrella.
All the people were saved
and none of them died.

Then he took a big breath and
blew all the fire out.
Everybody was safe—
safe and sound.
Everybody clapped Monster.
Then all the people said, "The
kids can go to the party now.
Monster has rescued the people
from the fire. People could
have been hurt."
Monster blew out the fire and
instead of all the people dying,
they lived for a long time.

All the parents let their
children go to Monster's
birthday party.
They said, "Hurrah for Monster!
Hurrah!"
Everybody went to Monster's
party. He had such a big smile
on his face.
Now everybody
could eat the cake.
Now everybody could burst
the balloons.

They went to the monster party
and played a lot of games.
The children played hide and
seek and Monster shut his
eyes and tried to find them.
"Hurrah, hurrah, for the
monster party," they all yelled.

Then they sang, "Monster's a jolly good fellow.
Monster's a jolly good fellow."
Monster was smiling a lot!